Robert Forbes Stewart

Faeries

Bumblebee Books
London

A CIP catalogue record for this title is
available from the British Library.

ISBN: 978-1-83934-295-0

Bumblebee Books is an imprint of
Olympia Publishers.

First Published in 2021

Bumblebee Books
Tallis House
2 Tallis Street
London
EC4Y 0AB

Printed in Great Britain

www.olympiapublishers.com

Dedication

I dedicate this book to my wife, Pauline.

Contents

The Corn Field

A little gust of wind came by,
And, in the ground, I spied groups of faeries bending straws
And chasing all the mice around.
Or were they chasing one another with the wind.
And bending straws that stood like masts of ships at anchor in the port?
The gust came by and with its breath
They went to hide away until a new event.

The Spooky Wood

Look, on a wall, an old stone wall, I saw a group of faeries stroll.
All in a line with soft footfall.
They went all in a row each one careful with their tread
So not to shake the rocky bed.
From crack to crevice, they came forth,
Many members following one another into
The dark and spooky wood.

The Farmer's Market

In the market, faeries find farmers selling cheese and wine.
All the treasure of the earth to keep faeries fit and fat,
Not too fat though, as if they were, they could not fly
To cottage gardens, where they like to go to watch things grow.
The market colors, so bright and gay, may be too bright
And frighten them away to coffee houses.
From stall to stall they go, where they like to nibble cheese
And taste the honey from the lid.
We miss seeing them because they are so small.

In the Pub

A dry day.
Faeries went into a pub, thirsty, they flittered in through side and back
Hiding into every nook and crack.
Into every glass they took a sip.
Look, where have they gone?
Maybe on whiskey trips to faerie land, on vapor trails with fiery wings.
They all came down in a circle, in a ring like a scorpion's sting.

A Walk with Faeries on the Beach

I walked with faeries on a beach, near to me, but out of reach.
They flittered down to the water's edge.
On the foam, they rode like swifts in the air,
Dipping and dodging they darted to and fro,
They came and went.
Some hid in shells.
They surfed the waves from crest to crest.
When they came back, their wings were wet, so, on the beach, They
stretched out to dry.
Some fell asleep.
Gulls came out with wicked greedy beaks,
Looking for a treat to eat, so, the faeries left on light feet.

Is the World Round or Flat?

I heard a little sound and put my ear close to the ground.
Faerie voices were arguing round and around I heard one say,
"The world is flat, so the world must have an edge,
The lines we draw are straight, they are not round and round.
If you stand here and I stand there,
We can pull a line between us and it is straight,
If the world was round, the line would curve around."
I think that faeries believe the world is flat.

Night-time

When night-time falls and bats come out,
The faeries can be seen around.
The moon leaves its mooring post and sails swiftly on the sea.
Faeries chase each other and laugh with glee.
They catch and tumble, oh so free!
Moonbeams give them light to see.
They have secrets we do not know,
Stories that they share with who?
Maybe a squirrel or a crow.
They riot about all wings aglow,
Then, into the night off they go,
Maybe to sleep.

A Drumming in the Air

Hark, I hear a drumming in the air,
Faeries are flying everywhere.
All about their wings spread out,
To find their place on flower heads or on the clover.
In the grass, they get tipsy on honeydew.
The fields there are a kaleidoscope of many colors,
Seed and flower heads of many a hue,
Here faeries drink this honeydew.
When in the meadows full of flowers,
We lie down and listen carefully for the sound of honeybees.
If we listen extremely hard, we can hear faerie wings drumming
And humming with the honeybees.

I Took Time Out

I took time out on a mossy wall to rest and think and watch
Night fall and the setting of the sun.
I think I saw faeries in a tree peeping out at me.
They like to hide and look at me.
Behind the leaves and twigs they hide.
They like to tease the squirrels.
They give their tails a tug and fly off to another tree.
Should I give the squirrels a hug?

Where the Rainbow Falls

Where sea grass and small flowers grow,
I think of little things that glow,
Like fireflies in the air or of faeries in the dunes
That know where little things will go.
They ride on reeds or on the surf,
They chase amongst the stones and shells,
To tumble down again or slide in the sand and bury faerie gold. They
flip and barrel in the air to maybe where the rainbow falls.

The Faerie Baker

The mist was rising from a field.
It cleared and I saw a wisp of smoke by an old oak tree rising high in the air.
It had a scent of burning, like crispy oak.
I went down to see the tiny oven in the roots of the tree and
Faeries there making bread from tiny grains of aniseed.
There a faerie baker, a little fat, had on his head a large white hat,
The roots of the tree were smoothed off for a faerie table
That nearly all could fit around.
The bread came out piping hot and when the lights came on
As night fell the faeries had a dance, a Wingatron.
They partied till the moon came out then they all flew off.
All about.

The Faerie Hills of Leitrim

In Leitrim, the hilltops hide many cavities.
In mounds and dells there are faerie rings and rows of stones,
Also pools, and streams and stranger things like lace webs that catch the dew.
Here faeries wash and make themselves anew,
To freshen wings and brighten shoes.
They do not need to climb the hills; they fly beneath the raven's wings.
In the mist that veil the hills, they sail and surf at will.
In the biggest hill lies a faerie fort for the king and queen.
From these rocky hollows, they fly out with their escort.

The Gossamer Threads Before the Snow

Faeries, why am I so suspicious of you?
You speak softly, you close my eyes,
You sneak into my brain with your stories.
I must write for you at your command, that you will be heard.
So, little people like you will fly to every corner and to every
Child feeding their imagination.
Have you found the internet?
Everyone does selfies or are glued to screens.
I think you can command the world for every generation still to come.
Will you digitalize them with so many dots?
Please, faeries, do not be so dotty. I know you love your selfies.
They make you so happy, will they fade with so millions more
On the world-wide net.

The May Fly Dance

Look, each ripple on the lake will say to other wavelets led astray,
"The faeries may come here today for the may-fly dance."
The colours of the rainbow show in a pattern to and fro.
Tiny flies dip and shoot across the lake trying to miss the fishes' gape.
Faeries are flying with so much fun we look to see and then they are gone.
A shower drove them all away, leaving more ripples on the lake today.
The wind has shaken the lake with its breath,
Rippling shores with lapping foam.
A gentle rhythm 'pitter patter' and all the faeries are driven back.

Moon Light and Shadows

The air was cool and still, gently poised for the night.
Was the snow waiting for the faeries visit so they could ride the drift?
And gently turn to float and spiral down,
To hide in the snow pillows built for the night's slumber-down.
After the night, all was quiet as we resume the quest
To find the secret of their private nest beneath the snow.
Is it a dark world?
They emerge from the drift as ice faeries.
Sometimes, indistinguishable from the snow,
So next time, when on snow do not step on the faeries sleeping deep below.

Winter

Where do faeries hide when the cold winds roar, and ice resides?
They may find a rock to hide behind or slip into a little nook. Behind a
door or cupboard, under a saucer there, or in a cup,
In the curtains they may wrap up.
They may sneak into the clothes we have hung up,
Or under beds or rugs they snuggle up.
Sometimes, they venture forth to cups, or mugs, for a little sup,
We see no faeries, as the night is dark, and they will flee.

Faerie Thieves

I look this way and that, even underneath the mat.
On the tabletop, and to every corner, I go,
It is not just here or there.
Every pencil that I buy, every key I want to use,
Every torch and tool I need is by faeries taken.
In their store put away by faerie greed.
Like their squirrel friends put away for a rainy day.
I watched them one by one creeping in behind my back on Faerie
feather feet they hide the loot behind their wings,
Then sneak into every crack and hole,
Sniggering at the things they took.

Faerie Games

This is for the strongest ones,
The fastest and for those that can jump the highest and longest.
Looking, I saw a faerie hitting hard another faerie in the yard.
I also saw another faerie fly like a jet across the sky.
There was a yard there, one meter long and one meter wide.
With little tracks on which they raced along with busy wings.
They ran long races and flew loopy patterns in the sky,
They tumbled high, they tumbled low.
Many claimed the races were not fair.
Some won stars for their vest and proudly flew high.
Their limbs were lean, their faces fair,
Their wings were bright and away they flew.

Faeries at Sea

You may not know but sometimes faeries
Can be seen at sea or stowing away on boats.
If you look up at the masts, they may be flying around
Chasing shadows of sails, or where sails used to be.
I have seen them chasing the spray or watching fish jump and
Hiding away from the gulls and the sailor's dogs and cats,
They watch the waves in the sea further from land
Than they would like to be.
When home from the sea,
They will go back home to a faerie tree.

The Faerie Tree

The tree is old, an old, old tree.
Within its bark it has faerie dust, magic dust.
For me this makes dreams sprinkled on the book of memory.
There are happy dreams, not sad ones which we forget.
The tree has many twists and turns, it is a gnarled and ancient thorn,
No one may take it away; it must always stay.
Each twist on stalk, or branch, or bough, will have its story.
A raven or crow will perch and talk to those that know.
Here, in troops the faeries go, circling the trunk to and fro.
Sometimes the mist will a blanket throw
Making a halo of mist for the faeries to dance below.
Some say that underneath, the roots trolls may go so,
Move the tree is a NO NO NO.

Faeries in the Shops

In some shops, faeries may be seen bright lights on their wings, Will
glitter giving them an incredibly special sheen.
Their colors are bright as they fly and giddily gad around.
In the windows, they are reflected so in this or that
One may see a fairy gliding by.
Patterns on clothes and frocks hide these faeries
Sneaking off with, or into socks.
Their shadows dance and flip.
Faeries on another trip like moths' hover and gather around
And without a sound move to another shop.

In the Supermarket

Faeries in shopping baskets like to hide,
Through the aisles they like to slide.
They can be found behind pots or tins
And in packets they may reside.
They move everything around to confuse the shoppers list. "Where is
this, where is that, I may need nuts for the cat."
Is this why when shopping I forget on returning home,
I miss what I did not get and blame the little folk.
They have many tricks I would like to bet.

Feeding Faeries

I put a little sugar on a twig
And press it beneath each mushroom head
Into the soft black earth where the faeries like to tread.
Like the hummingbirds of distant lands,
They need to speed their wings and grow.
I feed the faerie band.
Lightly they go stalk to flower head,
Their wings are strumming on the cold night air.
They fly one by one with so much care to find a moonbeam
For a trip into a house, or through leaf patterned trees
To dance on pools of light
For some of us to see.

At the Races

Faeries sometimes like to have a bet unless it rains and is very wet.
They go to see the horses run.
It has been known that, sometimes, the horses can be upset
When faeries fly too close and catch their eyes with faerie dust.
Then the horses may panic and throw their jockeys underfoot
As the horse tries to run away.
To be fair, I would not say that they cheat to make money from a bet.
They would like new stars to light them on their way.
They like to bet a lot.

The Faerie Printing Press

Faeries sometimes read the news in their leaflet press.
The press is working all day long.
It gossips and tells stories for the faerie throng.
It might be fake news for they like
To read of pussy cats and dogs and frogs.
And everything they need to know.
Some of them tell stories not quite right,
Of fashion fairies very thin and some that
Pose with smile a little fake and show off
Their pretty limbs and backside and belly.
They display their legs and arms and hands
In pretty patterns that they throw
With fluttering wings all for show.
The faerie printers working hard press the leaves
For the next edition of the 'Faerie Express'.

Faerie Fashion

The faeries are self-conscious about their looks.
Their favorite color is green.
This is why maybe sometimes they cannot be seen.
Yellow is the favorite color of the faerie queen as she likes to be seen.
Red is for the worker faeries.
They do not always work hard but like to spy on one another.
Some faeries are bullies and tease the little ones.
The faeries have a yearly fashion day.
They paint their wings with glitter, also their toes and nails.
In their fashion show, they dress in their brightest colors
And dress up and curl their hair.
They do not have a catwalk but have a wing walk.

The Faerie Bankers

We all like to buy and sell a lot, so do the faerie bankers.
They trade gold and silver grains of sand
They sell in every faerie house, hall, and land.
They give loans and, with their tricks, catch each faerie small and grand.
Caring not a jot if they need to lend a lot.
Stars can be bought, the faerie queen has already many of them.
She collects them to light up the sky.
She has far more stars than any others would be allowed to buy.
Far more than the king who owns a lot of sand.
The bankers are so prudent with their spoils they are so careful Not to lose a
grain, or drop a star.

The Hummingbirds

When days are warm, and little clouds chase one another across the sky
Take time to take a look closely on the ground.
There you may find a faerie drinking honey wine.
Some say the dew on the fat purple clover heads
Are the ones they like the best.
Nature provides this rich color to make the honey they need to fly.
They are like the hummingbirds of distant lands,
Or are those birds faeries in another guise?
Faeries will be fond of this disguise,
So butterflies and bees beware
There is competition here, so you need to be wise.

In the Orchard

When autumn comes around, there are fruits on many trees.
The apples and damsons have sweet fruit that faeries
Like to taste and where they like to be.
They particularly like the damsons sweet nectar.
They may get tipsy and roll around and do flips and falls
Or enjoy the rushing air on their wings.
They are unsteady when they get up to stroll
Away and roll down little hills.
They fall into ditches and get caught on hedges,
Maybe they need to sleep it off.
So, in the shadows, under trees, with the fallen fruit,
If you look closely there faeries you may see
With wings tucked up and under leaves,
Or in the fork of tree branches,
All so cosy warm as they can be.

The Moon Stone and the Harebell

One lucky faerie found a moon stone.
It was in fact an opal.
In these stones, there are many things
You may see countries, mountains, rivers - all the universe. Secretly
where he found it, he did not tell.
He collected more and more until he became like a banker,
An opal star banker, a rich star banker !
He became keeper of the opal bell.
He hid the secret with the hares
Because they were secretive and a little mad.
The other faeries were very jealous
And tried every trick to find the secret of the hare bell.
He had an idea to protect his find.
He told the hares to spread hare bells across the field so
No one would know which bell held the secret.

The Faerie Lamplighters

Down underground, in the caves, the lamp lighters go.
They sprinkle with light the tunnels all aglow with starshine
Lights to make a twinkling route where lost souls may go.
The starshine way goes with the river flow and finds its way to the castle,
Where the faerie king and queen hold their court.
To those who have fallen deep below the king and queen
Are particularly good to give them a way,
So none will be lost or go astray.
They keep a tight hold and master of all the faerie bands.

The Bright Sun

When the sun is very bright, and clouds have gone away,
The hills are dressed in blue and the water is mirror bright.
Then faeries will fly with their wings all a flicker
On the scattered light.
They rise in the warming air to share the days with butterflies.
They dance and glide and land with bright light feet
And shake their wings and show how fast they can go.
They will look to find new minds to share their thoughts
And gayly spread their joy, around
Then scatter like the autumn leaves.

The Faerie Guardians

There, a deserted house, a grey horse by the house wall,
In a park, a stump of an old tree long since rotted.
In this bygone estate, maybe the horse has a memory of being
Underneath the tree, which was once a fine old tree,
Or a memory of his stable and of the people he once knew.
I wonder do faeries bring back to him the world wherein he grew?
The house is gone, it's window blind.
A roof barely hangs on a grey walled world and the friends
He heard long since gone away.
Next door in our busy world, we race on.
We dream to fill and flee this lonely world with our kindness
And thoughts of the friends we once knew.
Our memory is with the faerie guardians of this lonely house.

A Country Walk in the Hills

I took a country walk to the hills.
The old black and white dog was in the tractor shed beside the lane.
The lane is lined with old moss deep covered walls.
Birds in their best dress flip from rock-to-rock bobbing on the brow.
Grey crows play hop, skip and jump from rock-to-rock.
The sky is moving, shaking out its duvet and pillows
In grey and white high and rounded clouds like the hills.
Light breezes wave the grasses along the old stone track.
The old dog is with the faeries in his dreams.
Here he is running free in the hills
And smelling many scents on the mountain air.

Faeries in France

Do faeries go abroad?
Although I think they like to stay,
Maybe they have a bucket list and like to go away.
They like to hitch a lift, so, they will not go astray.
I was surprised when, in Auvergne,
I saw faeries that had probably stowed away.
I viewed the volcanos now extinct in roller coaster rows
Some like peaked high or tricorn hats.
Behind the dark cathedrals and churches,
Lies a town where they could fly from roof to roof
And steeple top and there also to hide.
Do they fly here to warm their wings?
There is no lava flow, but the volcano tops present a view
That they will certainly enjoy.
They will warm in the sunny clime of France.

Golden Light

Here we see the light filled landscape of the drumlin hills.
The luminous sky is deep with water clouds.
Do we find the cattle in the fields pointing all the same way?
Watching the little faerie folk?
The trees are adorned with golden evening light.
The faeries have disappeared into the shadows
Because of the low light.
Like the shadows that flicker through the mind.
Memories come and go faerie winged.
They move so fast they cannot be caught
But eternally feed the imagination.

Starlight

Some say faeries are made from the dust of stars.
When shadows play in the light of night
And shooting stars cross the heaven's sea,
We look up and feel free as we roam the sky above.
Here on the earth, the half-light may reveal patterns of faerie lights.
Little shapes lightly passing through the night like moths
Scattered here and there and through the moving branches of the trees,
Not resting but moving like the water light of streams.
Not quite transparent but nearly so
With no weight they pass on moon light shoes.

Panthers on the Prowl

At night, the black panthers are on the prowl for faerie folk.
With their yellow eyes, they pierce the dark and show danger
As they sniff to find a prey and pounce on the little folk,
They are silent with their tread.
The wasps and the bees that own the day
Seek nectar from flower and tree.
They carry with them their lances to sting the little folk
Who might get too close?
So, faeries stay alive from the silent hunters of the day and night.

In African Lands

In African lands, where the lions roam faeries are scarce,
Here they do not feel at home, the sun is too hot.
They must rest on the backs of elephants
Or way up high with the giraffes to lift them up to the sky.
On their horns, this is a super spot for selfies either alone or in groups.
They can fly to tall trees, and tickle monkeys
Who then think they have fleas.
They avoid crocodiles, buffalos and the hippopotamus
With its mighty gape.
They avoid the swamps that teem with snakes and birds with long beaks,
These are places where faeries never frequent.
They would not dare.
Soon they are glad to come home.

Faeries Lost

Sometimes, faeries do get lost.
In high winds, they cannot fly unless with the wind or flying very high.
I found one on a corner looking lost waiting for I do not know who.
I went on my journey and on returning,
There he was with wings and feet tucked up so small and sad.
His friends, the faerie band, had left him all alone
Forgetting to count the numbers of their group, they had flown away.
A small dog said to him,
"Jump up on me, I know where they are,
I saw them fly to the shops full of excitement.
There, they could ride on trolleys and eat the crumbs
From the shoppers' bags as they walked and gossiped
With their friends to their cars."
The small dog carried the faerie back to the faerie band.
As the rain was spitting, they flew back to the woods.
Be careful when you are shopping, when you load up
There is no faerie in your car.

A Walk in the Woods

I like to walk in the woods to watch the birds and squirrels.
I like to walk with autumn leaves on a softly colored path
Of yellow brown or red.
Leaves that will quieten my tread with their gentle hues.
I like to walk with my thoughts and with my faerie guides
That are here with me.
They come waving fans of peacefulness to cool my mind
And let it wander free.
Upon a pool, I see bright light, an echo of the sky.
It is a pool for the hogs or forest dwellers,
A present from the clouds, a cup to drink or plunder from.
The trees deep underground it may feed.
Also, a stream where faeries swim.

Crossing the Stream

I look carefully at a stream that is slipping by.
I climb the faerie steps and see within the river run pebbles in patterns.
Some close in rows for faerie feet to cross.
I wondered how and where did those faeries come from?
Do they fall from trees, or are they blown from thistle down?
Or from the early morning mist as in the trails of shifting clouds?
We are surprised by faerie forms in the light that comes
And goes on the snows, or in flocks of bird like murmurations.
Maybe they come in the spray of waterfalls!
They dance with the light, an awesome sight.
No, I think they come from faeries dells where flowers open
To the light casting their beauty in a throng.

The Moon Beam

As night deepens the moon comes out full of light, it has risen.
The moonbeams fall steep between curtain and glass.
They fall on the little children deep in sleep.
Faeries down the moonbeams creep
With their little wings so fast asleep,
Down they come to safely keep all the little ones now fast asleep.
Down they come, one by one,
To dance around on moonlight feet.
We look again and they are gone back up the moonbeams,
One by one.

Sunrise

When the wide spreading light comes up,
Is it time to go to a wing danceatron?
Then the faeries feather flip and glide and chase away the shadows.
The sun's warm glare is for the faeries fare fun,
They like to bask in the warm days air and chase butterflies
And hover over flower heads.
Faeries where do you hide? Or why do you hide?
We like to see you glide and fly about,
Maybe you are shy and like to keep your secrets to yourself
And make a mystery for us?
We are all homed in the universe of many stars
And would like to feel at home with your faerie band
And fly away with you to another land.

The Faerie Jeweler

When berries are ripe on the bush and pebbles are washed
In streams running clear,
It gives the faerie jeweler materials that are free.
With her craft, she makes bright jewels for fashion.
These are created for the 'little folk'.
She makes little chains and rings
From golden grass tempered by the wind,
Or with grains of golden sand which maybe come
From precious stones: jewels from the rock and earth.
So, when you lie on the grass and make daisy chains
And investigate the clear blue sky with its pale moon
And golden sun, think of the faerie jeweler.
With her busy fingers making the finest things,
As fine as the spider's lace or the gossamer dew,
Or the patterns of lichens in the clear blue air.

The Faerie Houses in the Wood

The yew tree stood deep in the wood.
It was dark and high, and, after many years,
His arms spread wide.
He was guardian for the faerie troop.
They walked on a path with shadows on either side.
Here and there where shapes like dinner plates,
So white were they that they stood out and were a shock to see.
These were mushrooms which roofed the houses of the faeries.
In the wood, there were many types of every tree and,
As you passed a corner on the path ferns
Dressed all the rocks with their canopy.
The wood was so dark and deep,
The sun only shyly cast its dappled spots,
That came and went, moving all the time.
Faerie forms could be there but then,
We may not see in such a dark and spooky wood.

Faerie Skaters

When icy ponds are frozen white
And the surrounding trees are frosty bright,
Faeries like to skate at night.
They ghost upon the glass and slide,
With wings stretched out they fly and play,
They chase and race until the last light of day.
Maybe they are chasing the night away.
When light comes up, their reflections they can see.
Now is the time for faeries to flee.
Possibly into the arms of a friendly tree to wrap up in leaves,
Close their wings and, with their heads tucked up,
They gather to keep warm all together.

Faerie Paths

In grassy dells if you look well into the grass, deep inside,
You may see where faeries pass lightly.
They make little paths where mushrooms grow.
When, in darkness, or in rain, or in snow,
The caps of yellow white and red and patterned tops will show
A path, so, they will know where to go.
Perhaps to a faerie tree or down to faerie castles that lie deep below.
(That is why mushrooms often grow in lines)

The Hermit and the Faerie

A faerie heard that there was a hermit nearby.
The faerie was curious.
She knew that hermits choose to be alone
As they like to live in their minds.
Their life is about another world,
They are not aliens but need space and time to think and think.
To find peace for their thoughts,
To fly and find a universal thing or new ways
Into the universe of the mind.
This hermit had only one possession, an incandescent pearl.
He was very fond of it and it rolled away from him
When he fell asleep meditating.
The pearl then found a place in the sky.

The faerie came by and asked, "Why are you so cross?
I thought you were at peace!"

As hermits cannot have possessions
So, nothing more was said.
However, the faerie saw that the hermit was sad
Because he had lost his pearl.
The faerie said,
"I have found a pearl and I played roller-coaster with it.
It is very beautiful, so, I will give it back to you."

The faerie thought this was the kindest thing to do.
She, then, flew off as he did not want to be the hermits' pet. Later the
faerie returned.

"Tell me about your sadness," the faerie asked.
"What do you mean?" the hermit said, "there are no sadness." "Have
you no regrets, or things that you have lost?
Like the pearl of wisdom that I found for you?" asked the faerie.
"Faeries or people cannot lose something that they will never have,
Because they are too busy," the hermit said.
"All things have to come and go,
Going might be the most interesting, so, we have no loss."
"You are not cross with me coming to see you,"
Asked the faerie.
"Maybe knowing too much is a bad thing," said the hermit. "Because
then, we become blind to the beauty around us."

"But what if we lose our sight and cannot see?" asked the faerie.
"This doesn't matter, because all these beautiful things,
Once we have seen them, they stay with us,
Within our imagination," replied the hermit.
"Then should I not be so busy?" asked the faerie.
"Yes, this is a good idea, the best solution so we have more time here
To be kind and not regret our time here.
With our kindnesses and not regret we are here.
Listen to the running water and look to the clouds
That puff across the sky.
As if we are on a train, on a peaceful journey to a happy end,"
Said the hermit.

The Hermit's Story

I was getting older and people did ugly things
Like go to war and become racist.
They were nasty and not kind to one another.
They were greedy and cheated one another with lies and money,
Thinking that money made them important,
Particularly if they had more of it than anyone else.
I was so distressed that all my good ideas were considered unimportant,
That I sought shelter within the rocks.
These could tell me stories and history: these are precious things.
Stones can tell us why we are here and give us the heavens' music,
So, I am never lonely but always amazed by all these splendors.

Look how bright is the edge of the clouds?
They are constantly in motion!
These plumes of light drift above us.
They are up there
With the sunlight and the wind.
They cruise over our troubled world.
The icy clouds are changing like our short journey,
They come and go in this world.

Hide and Seek

As shadows flee with the moon's swift feet,
The faeries chase one another, they play 'hide and seek'.
If I am very quiet and sneak up on them,
I will be able to see how they fly,
Their busy little wings make a humming in the air.
They flit so fast we can hardly see.
Is that a bee or a faerie behind me?
Is this a trick or a shadow of the moon?
Its fleeting friends that tease the land in hollows and on hills
And gives a panoply to entertain the eye, oops!
It is cold when the moon peeps out behind its cloudy curtain.

The Fiddler in the Dell

A lane (boreen) leads to a fairy hill.
It passes by a dell framed by apple trees.
I passed along it and heard a sweet sound.
The trees were in blossom, it was indeed a beautiful day.
I was curious to hear where the sound was coming from.
I peered over the wall to the faerie dell and there,
I saw a ring of small people (faerie) listening to the tunes of a fiddler.
The figures were dressed in clothes made from leaves
And spring flower petals.
I listened as the pace of music increased.
Enthralled, I found my conscience slipping away
Into the vision of more and more
Little people coming from the woods.
Animals came to listen to the hypnotizing music.
I fell asleep with these tunes inside my head.
When I awoke, all the little folk were gone and I left the dell
With the scent and sound of spring.

What Winter can we expect?

What winter can we expect?
We seek our warmth from the fireplace or a cozy rug.
Our clothes barely keep us warm.
The running water feeds the dry parchment of the earth
For a bed of rest.
We have had enough of autumns clock.
We watch the falling leaves. Where did that leaf go?
We look again. Did a faerie run away with one?
The leaves are in their autumn dance, they lift, swirl,
Chase and twirl with the wind.
They have fallen as autumn's golden shawl
From trees lit by the lower sun.
The gold is deep and warm, as any golden ring.
The sky is cool, blue, and fresh after the rain.

About the Author

Robert Forbes Stewart was born in Oxford in 1944. He was an art lecturer in Sligo, Ireland for eighteen years. He retired early to concentrate on his art and small farm in county Leitrim, Ireland. He, together with his artist wife, Pauline, ran a small craft shop/gallery in Sligo town. He has participated in many solo and group exhibitions in Ireland and abroad. He has two sons and grandchildren.

Acknowledgements

I thank my son, Daragh, for his help with design and layout.
My grandson, Charlie, for collating the text.
My wife, Pauline, for editing

Printed in Great Britain
by Amazon

82576635R30065